*For Rory
& Conor*

First published 1997 by Walker Books Ltd, 87 Vauxhall Walk, London SE11 5HJ

2 4 6 8 10 9 7 5 3 1

© 1997 Penny Dale

This book has been typeset in Garamond ITC Book.

Printed in Italy

British Library Cataloguing in Publication Data
A catalogue record for this book is available from the British Library.

ISBN 0-7445-4935-3

Big Brother, Little Brother

Penny Dale

WALKER BOOKS

AND SUBSIDIARIES

LONDON • BOSTON • SYDNEY

When Little Brother cries like this,
who knows why?

Big Brother.

"He wants to eat the same food as me.

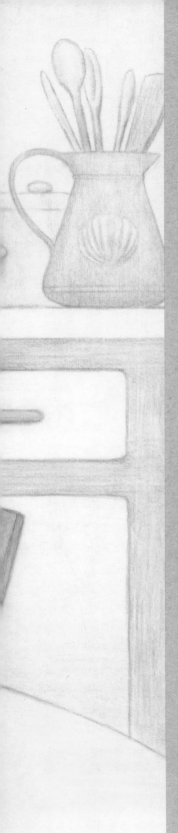

See, I knew, didn't I?"

When Little Brother looks like this,
who knows why?

Big Brother.

"He wanted you to take the dog away.
He's scared.

See, I knew, didn't I?"

When Little Brother shouts like this,
who knows why?

Big Brother.

"He wants to be in here with me.

See, I knew, didn't I?"

But when
Little Brother
wants
Big Brother's
truck ...

what
does
Big Brother
say?

"No!
You can't
have it.
It's mine."

When Big Brother puts his truck away,

and Little Brother takes it,

and Big Brother can't find it,

Big Brother starts to cry.

When Big Brother cries like this,
who knows why?

Little Brother.

"You knew.
You brought me back my truck.

We're brothers, that's why."